# Ted and Tim

# The Sound of T

by Cecilia Minden and Joanne Meier · illustrated by Bob Ostrom

# The Child's World

Published by The Child's World®
1980 Lookout Drive
Mankato, MN 56003-1705
800-599-READ
www.childsworld.com

The Child's World®: Mary Berendes, Publishing Director
The Design Lab: Design and page production

Library of Congress Cataloging-in-Publication Data
Minden, Cecilia.
  Ted and Tim : the sound of T / by Cecilia Minden and
Joanne Meier ; illustrated by Bob Ostrom.
     p. cm.
  ISBN 978-1-60253-417-9 (library bound : alk. paper)
  1. English language—Consonants—Juvenile literature.
2. English language—Phonetics—Juvenile literature. 3.
Reading—Phonetic method—Juvenile literature. I. Meier,
Joanne D. II. Ostrom, Bob. III. Title.
  PE1159.M575 2010
  [E]—dc22                                    2010005608

Printed in the United States of America in Mankato, MN.
July 2010
F11538

## NOTE TO PARENTS AND EDUCATORS:

The Child's World® has created this series with the goal of exposing children to engaging stories and illustrations that assist in phonics development. The books in the series will help children learn the relationships between the letters of written language and the individual sounds of spoken language. This contact helps children learn to use these relationships to read and write words.

The books in this series follow a similar format. An introductory page, to be read by an adult, introduces the child to the phonics feature, or sound, that will be highlighted in the book. Read this page to the child, stressing the phonic feature. Help the student learn how to form the sound with her mouth. The story and engaging illustrations follow the introduction. At the end of the story, word lists categorize the feature words into their phonic elements.

Each book in this series has been carefully written to meet specific readability requirements. Close attention has been paid to elements such as word count, sentence length, and vocabulary. Readability formulas measure the ease with which the text can be read and understood. Each book in this series has been analyzed using the Spache readability formula.

Reading research suggests that systematic phonics instruction can greatly improve students' word recognition, spelling, and comprehension skills. This series assists in the teaching of phonics by providing students with important opportunities to apply their knowledge of phonics as they read words, sentences, and text.

**This is the letter t.**

In this book, you will read words that have the **t** sound as in: *toy, tag, team,* and *teacher.*

Ted and Tim are brothers.

They like to do
things together.
They play toy trains.

They climb trees.

They ride on the tire swing.

They like to play tag.

They play on the same team.

Ted is number ten.

Tim is number two.

They take turns kicking
the ball.

They have the same teacher.

Her name is Miss Topper.

Which one is Tim?

Which one is Ted?

Ted is tall.

Tim has a missing tooth.

It is fun to be

brothers together.

# Fun Facts

Do you like sports? If the answer is yes, then you probably have played on a team at some point. In baseball, nine members of each team are on the field during a play. In football and field hockey, that number is eleven, and in basketball, it is five.

Have you ever lost a tooth? All kids lose about 20 primary teeth (also called baby teeth) between the ages of 5 and 13. By adulthood, most people have a set of 32 permanent teeth. This is less than several other creatures, including dogs and pigs. Dogs have 42 teeth, and pigs have 44.

# Activity

### Relay Racing with Two Teams

Do you enjoy racing? If so, invite your friends over for a day of relay races. You will need to divide into two teams. Races might include running from one point to another, dribbling a basketball between two plastic cones, or even hopping back and forth in a potato sack! Members of the winning team get to decide what the next relay race will be. Be sure to take breaks between races and to drink plenty of water so you stay energized.

# To Learn More

## Books
### About the Sound of T
Moncure, Jane Belk. *My "t" Sound Box®*. Mankato, MN: The Child's World, 2009.

### About Teams
Bailey, Linda, and Bill Slavin (illustrator). *The Farm Team*. Kids Can Press, 2006.

Shaw, Fran, and Ryuichi Sakamoto (illustrator). *What a Team!: Together Everyone Achieves More*. Pleasantville, NY: Readers' Digest Children's Books, 2007.

### About Teeth
Lane, Jeanette, and Carolyn Bracken (illustrator). *The Magic School Bus and the Missing Tooth*. New York: Scholastic, 2006.

Miller, Edward. *The Tooth Book: A Guide to Healthy Teeth and Gums*. New York: Holiday House, 2008.

### About Togetherness
Holzschuher, Cynthia. *Play Together, Share Together: Fun Activities for Parents and Children*. Westminster, CA: Teacher Created Materials, 2000.

Simmons, Jane. *Together*. New York: A.A. Knopf, 2007.

## Web Sites
### Visit our home page for lots of links about the Sound of T:
*childsworld.com/links*

Note to Parents, Teachers, and Librarians: We routinely check our Web links to make sure they're safe, active sites—so encourage your readers to check them out!

# T Feature Words

## Proper Names
Ted
Tim
Topper

## Feature Words in Initial Position
tag
take
tall
teacher
team
ten
tire
to
together
tooth
toy
turn
two

## Feature Words with Blends
train
tree
bright
brother

24

## About the Authors

Cecilia Minden, PhD, is the former director of the Language and Literacy Program at the Harvard Graduate School of Education. She is now a reading consultant for school and library publications. She earned her PhD in reading education from the University of Virginia. Cecilia and her husband, Dave Cupp, live outside Chapel Hill, North Carolina. They enjoy sharing their love of reading with their grandchildren, Chelsea and Qadir.

Joanne Meier, PhD, has worked as an elementary school teacher, university professor, and researcher. She earned her BA in early childhood education from the University of South Carolina, and her MEd and PhD in education from the University of Virginia. She currently works as a literacy consultant for schools and private organizations. Joanne lives in Virginia with her husband Eric, daughters Kella and Erin, two cats, and a gerbil.

## About the Illustrator

Bob Ostrom has been illustrating children's books for nearly twenty years. A graduate of the New England School of Art & Design at Suffolk University, Bob has worked for such companies as Disney, Nickelodeon, and Cartoon Network. He lives in North Carolina with his wife Melissa and three children, Will, Charlie, and Mae.